Just in Time, ABRAHAM LINCOLN

Patricia Polacco

PUFFIN BOOKS
An Imprint of Penguin Group (USA) Inc.

When Michael walked into the double sleeper on the Amtrak Limited bound for Washington, D.C., he said, "This is too cool!"

"Way cool," Derek echoed.

But when the boys were pulling their bedclothes out of their knapsacks, iPods, cell phones and video games tumbled out onto the floor.

"Oh no," their grandmother scolded. "No electronics on this trip—no music, no texting, no tweeting, no e-mailing."

"Then what are we going to do?" the boys howled.

"Do? Well, that's something of a secret, but first stop will be Harpers Ferry, West Virginia, where there is someone I want you both to meet."

Derek slipped his lucky penny from his pocket. "I can keep this, can't I?" he asked.

His grandmother smiled and nodded yes.

The next morning, after they ate breakfast, the train stopped in Harpers Ferry. As it lurched to a stop, a very tall man met them on the platform.

"Mr. Portufoy!" their grandma sang out. "Here are the two grandsons I was telling you about.

"Mr. Portufoy has a marvelous collection of Civil War uniforms, rifles and a wondrous display of the photographs of Mathew Brady and his photographers!"

"Who's Mathew Brady?" Derek asked.

"Aw, everybody knows that. . . . He's the dude that took pictures of battlegrounds during the Civil War." Michael yawned. "We studied him in class."

Mr. Portufoy, their grandma whispered to them, was a "true expert" on the Civil War. The boys looked at each other, bored.

After tea, Mr. Portufoy and their grandmother took the boys to the museum. It was dusty. The Mathew Brady photographs were black and white and definitely boring, one of President Lincoln and some general just standing there.

Then they saw the weapons used in the Civil War—guns and cannons, bayonets and cannonballs.

"Man," Michael exclaimed, running from case to case. "It must have been cool to fight in that war!"

"Way cool," Derek said.

"So you think the Civil War was cool, do you?" Mr. Portufoy mused, and looked at their grandma.

Michael didn't answer. He was eyeing one particularly splendid uniform.

Mr. Portufoy came up behind him. "I have some very authentic uniforms packed away in the archives. Would you like to try one on?"

For the first time since they'd come to Harpers Ferry, the boys smiled. "Would we!" Derek said.

In the archive room, Mr. Portufoy opened an old chest and set out two blue uniforms. "Do you boys know which side used these uniforms?"

"Union!" Michael shouted out. From his history class he knew that the war had been fought between the North and the South because they couldn't agree on slavery. He knew Northern soldiers wore blue, Southern soldiers—called Confederates—wore gray.

Mr. Portufoy began buttoning up the uniform on Derek. "And did you know that President Abraham Lincoln came right here to Harpers Ferry on his way to Antietam?"

"What's Antietam?" Michael asked. He knew about Abraham Lincoln.

"Antietam was one of the most unforgettable battles of the Civil War."

"Hey, I had a video game about the battle of Gettysburg," Derek chirped. "I blew away four hundred soldiers all by myself. I think I set a record."

"Well," Mr. Portufoy said thoughtfully, "how would you like to play something better than a video game? A real game. One that might even take courage!"

"Can we keep the uniforms on?" Michael asked.

"Oh, yes. You *have* to keep the uniforms on . . . that's part of the game."

"Do we get swords and guns?" Derek asked excitedly.

"No swords or guns."

"We don't get to shoot anyone?" Michael whined.

Mr. Portufoy stooped down and took the boys' shoulders. "You are going to Antietam just after the battle. You are going to eat what soldiers eat, walk where they walk, see what they see." Then he looked up at a giant wooden door. "When you walk through that door, you will be in the middle of the . . . game."

He took something gold out of his pocket. "I'm giving you this pocket watch, Michael. Guard this with your life. When you hear the watch chime, you have one hour to get back to this door before sunset. One rule: You cannot tell any of the other players who you really are, nor anything about your modern life. You are young soldiers and it is 1862."

The boys nodded a cautious yes, and Mr. Portufoy nudged them through the door. Their grandmother was nowhere in sight.

On the other side, they were standing right next to their hotel . . . but it was dark. "Whoa," said Derek. "The sun was shining, it was almost lunchtime. Now it's night!"

"Look, Derek," Michael whispered. "No cars. No electric lights, only torchlights."

A small horse-drawn wagon came trotting up and stopped right next to them. "Where've you two been?" an angry voice called out at them. "I've been waiting for you for well nigh an hour!" The boys climbed in and realized they were piled in with stacks of glass photographers' plates and a great big standing camera.

"Derek, that's Mathew Brady!" Michael whispered even though he knew this was just a game.

They stopped in front of a shop that read Photographic Studio. There was already a carriage and a group of soldiers waiting.

"Collect the equipment," the photographer barked. "Load it into the carriage."

But when they came into the store, there was a very tall man in a cape and a tall hat. When he removed his hat, the boys gasped.

"Michael," Derek whispered, "where did they get someone who looks so much like Abraham Lincoln?"

"Mr. President," Mr. Brady said, as he gave him a slight bow. "An honor."

"Mr. Brady, sir, your reputation precedes you. I understand that one of your photographers will photograph my meeting with General McClellan, celebrating the Northern victory at Antietam."

"One of the best, sir."

Wow! Michael thought. What a game!

In the carriage, as it jiggled along, two soldiers sent by General McClellan gave the boys small packets they called "jerky." "It's the last you'll have for some time, boy," one said. Michael thought it tasted like shoe leather.

Then, the two soldiers got to whispering about the battle. How it lasted one day. How thousands of soldiers clashed in a cornfield. How the Northerners met Confederates posted along a sunken road the two soldiers were calling "Bloody Lane."

"Course, it weren't called that until two days ago," one trooper said, his voice breaking.

The other soldier's eyes began to tear. "Those boys walked across that cornfield as if they were invincible. But they weren't."

These soldiers sure talked real. Michael could feel his heart beating through his uniform. Good thing it was just a game.

Mr. Lincoln said not a word. By daybreak they rolled into the encampment at Antietam. When Lincoln climbed out, he chucked Derek under the chin. "I been watching you, boy. You remind me greatly of my boy, Willie." He turned and followed the two troopers.

"Whoever this guy is, he's really good," Derek said.

"You there, boys!" It was the Brady photographer. Already here. He grabbed a camera out of the carriage.

"Alexander Gardner's the name!" he barked. "We gotta use this morning sun." The boys hustled after him across a pasture. A battlefield?

The pattern was always the same: first, by foot, Gardner would search for the picture he wanted, then he'd call for his camera, set the picture up, take it, and move on. He photographed a field of broken cornstalks littered with torn blue caps. He photographed a tree, whose branches were exploded away.

"Here, boy," he'd shout, and Derek or Michael would run to hand him another glass plate. But where were the soldiers, Confederate or Union? What kind of game was this? They said the battle had been over for two days; did the soldiers just go home when the game was over?

But then the photographer moaned, "Oh, my God! Over here." Through a small woods, he'd come upon a low hill with a shed on it. Then Michael saw what the photographer saw: Behind the shed were three soldiers, one sitting, one on his side as if he were swimming, stiff and not moving. Two wore blue, one wore gray.

Beyond them in the distance were more soldiers lying still, as if they were sleeping. And a soldier with a wagon moving around, collecting them.

Michael sat down on the plowed ground, the wind knocked out of him. "Derek," he whispered. "I don't understand it, but this is no game."

"Your first battlefield?" a voice asked sadly. The boys nodded. It was President Lincoln!

He put his hands on their shoulders.

"A terrible thing . . . war." His voice trailed off. "Twenty-three thousand men dead or wounded.

"I can only wonder as I stand here today if it is worth this dreadful sacrifice. . . . My heart breaks that I ordered these lads to their death." He spoke as he walked the boys back to the encampment.

Michael looked at his watch. It was already 3:00! "Derek! The clock hasn't chimed. How can we make it back to Harpers Ferry in time to get through the door by sunset?"

Derek started to cry. "It doesn't matter, Michael. Don't you see—we're here, really here! In the middle of the Civil War. We'll never see Gramma again."

"My dear boys . . . you should have never been out on that battlefield," Mr. Lincoln said as he walked them toward McClellan's tent.

He hugged them both.

"If only I could be assured that all of this death, destruction and loss is worth the price."

Michael could feel the president's heart breaking.

He suddenly knelt in front of him, and it burst out of him. "But Mr. Lincoln, the North is going to win the war. The country will stay together." He caught himself. The game. Mr. Portufoy's one rule. He couldn't tell Mr. Lincoln how he knew!

"If only I could be assured of that, boy," the president whispered. "If only I could be assured that slavery will be abolished and the Union restored, one voice, one country . . . one nation." Mr. Lincoln's eyes seemed as sad as time.

"But it is true, Mr. Lincoln," Derek suddenly sputtered. "We know. We're from the future. You have to believe us! The North is going to win."

"America will become a powerful nation," Michael whispered, forgetting all about Mr. Portufoy's rules.

"And one day, Mr. Lincoln"—Derek was almost smiling—"a black man will become president!"

"A black man, president!" Mr. Lincoln looked at him, the slightest smile at the corner of his mouth. "A black man president. . . . But where . . . why . . . how are you boys even here at Antietam?"

"It was a game, Mr. Lincoln. Or it was supposed to be, but it wasn't," Derek answered. He started to sob. Mr. Lincoln put his arms around him.

"War is anything but a game, my boy." He was looking straight in Derek's eyes now and took his hand. "I lost my son Will last February from typhoid. A beautiful boy just as you are. I feel that same spirit in you. Foolish, but maybe he sent you to me."

"Wait, Mr. Lincoln. I have proof, my lucky penny—look, it's you . . . look at the date. 2007."

Just then, the photographer Gardner came up behind them. "Look lively, boys, we have to photograph the president and the general . . . the light is just right."

Derek stuffed his lucky penny back into his pocket.

Michael handed glass plate after glass plate to Gardner, then stood back with Derek, as the photographer photographed the general and the president standing. The general and the president sitting.

When he was finished, Gardner bowed. "Thank you, sirs," he said, gathered his equipment and left. President Lincoln walked slowly over to the boys.

The late-afternoon sun was low in the sky; it was getting late. Michael held out

his watch. "When this watch chimes, sir, we have only an hour to get back to Harpers Ferry. But it's so late. We have to leave now."

Without hesitation, Lincoln called one of McClellan's troopers. "These boys need to get back to Harpers Ferry before nightfall. Please advise the general."

Relieved, Michael came up to the president. "Sir, you will go down in history as one of the greatest presidents of the United States that ever lived."

"My, my." Mr. Lincoln smiled warmly at them for a long moment, then he shook both of their hands. "Hurry now, lads. The driver is waiting."

The sun sat on the ridge of pine trees and the horses were galloping along the road when Michael felt the pocket watch finally chime. "We're not going to make it," Derek screamed in panic.

"Sir." Michael leaned into the window. "Is there a faster way to Harpers Ferry?"

"Yes, cross-country!" the soldier shouted back. "May not be safe. Enemy troops."

Michael didn't hesitate. "Let's do it!"

The driver handed back muskets to the boys. "You know how to fire these?"

Derek started to answer no, but Michael nudged him, and they both signaled yes. "Be on the ready."

For the next while there was no trouble. Then, just as they rounded a bend in the road on a cliff above the Potomac River, they heard war whoops coming from the woods on their right flank.

"All right, Derek, raise your musket, get ready to fire," Michael shouted.

"But, Michael, I can't. I don't know how!" Derek whined.

Then, the coach lurched over and skidded onto its side. The horses broke loose and ran.

The boys were dazed for a time, but when they looked up, on the side of a valley just across the Potomac, they could see little houses nestled. Harpers Ferry!

"We have to run for it! Let's go!"

The boys ran and ran until they could taste blood in the backs of their throats. Finally, they bolted across the rail bridge that leads into Harpers Ferry. Union troops were guarding it, but when they saw the uniforms the boys were wearing, they let them pass.

Finally they ran up the last hill to the door of the museum. But Michael looked at his watch. He sat down in a heap. "It's been more than an hour! We didn't make it, Derek." Michael pulled at the door. Game or not, it was locked. It wouldn't open.

Both boys sat on the doorstep, rocking and crying.

"We're never gonna see Gramma again," Derek sobbed. "We're stuck in 1862—should we have warned Mr. Lincoln about the theater?"

"No, Derek—giving him hope was fine, but if we had told him that, it could have changed history."

At exactly that moment, the door unlatched and squeaked open, spilling the bright lights of the museum onto the alley where they were sitting. They turned.

"You broke the rules," they heard a stern voice say. Mr. Portufoy!

"But some rules are meant to be broken."

At the hotel, the boys ran all the way to their grandmother's room and leapt into her arms.

"You boys act like you haven't seen me in ages. You've only been gone an hour!"

Michael breathed a deep sigh. It had been a game after all. Mr. Lincoln, the battleground, the escape. All of it.

"But Gramma," Derek insisted, "we were really there. At Antietam! We saw dead soldiers, battlefields . . . we saw President Lincoln!"

"Oh, boys, what you took part in was a Reenactment. Entire groups all around the country put on uniforms and act out important battles of the war," their grandmother reassured them.

"No, Gramma, we were there," Derek said.

Their grandmother thought for a time.

"Well, boys, if whatever you experienced made history come to life for you, then that is all that counts!" she crowed.

That afternoon after tea in the museum, the two boys went over to the Civil War photos. There it was, the one by Alexander Gardner: President Lincoln and General McClellan standing in front of the tent.

Michael paused, because there in the background, almost in the shadows, were two boys.

"Gramma . . . come look!" the boys gasped.

Their grandmother came over to the photo.

She adjusted her glasses, her eyes widened, she reeled back.

For there on that wall in the Civil War photo, very clearly, were Michael and Derek.

MY DEAR READERS,

At the Battle at Antietam, September 17, 1862, the Union and Confederate armies together suffered the greatest losses for one day of any Civil War battle—23,000 dead and wounded.

It was a battle General Robert E. Lee could have won. But he didn't, all because of a paper wrapped around three cigars! Just weeks before Antietam, Lee had stood up to the Union army at the Second Battle of Bull Run. Now his goal was to move west and encounter the Union army in the North itself—Maryland! The South was running short of supplies, fall was coming on; if Lee could defeat the Union soldiers in the North, he could raid Northern farms and get much-needed food supplies. Indeed, such a victory would mean a real turning point to the whole war.

But a Union soldier discovered the cigars, opening up the paper covering them to discover that it showed where Lee planned to station his troops at Antietam. The soldier rushed the information to General George McClellan, and this crucial information gave McClellan and the Union army extraordinary advantage.

The actual one-day battle occurred near the village of Sharpsburg at Antietam Creek. A sunken road where the Confederates got trapped became Bloody Lane. A major battleground, one that I have pictured, was a simple cornfield, which in the days that followed became forever after The Cornfield.

My story telescopes time. No one really won the battle at Antietam conclusively. General Lee sent his entire Army of Northern Virginia into action—38,000 soldiers, and even though General McClellan had the cigar-paper information about Lee's plans, McClellan cautiously only sent two thirds of his army into the battle—60,000. It was not enough for a total victory. McClellan would lose his position as commander in chief for this decision. But not for another three months. The actual day that Lincoln visited McClellan and the battlefield was October 3, nearly two weeks after the battle. The two armies would have gathered their wounded and their dead long before that.

Perhaps this story, then, was indeed a reenactment where time can be telescoped, as the grandmother of Derek and Michael said. Or perhaps it was a game like no other, where the magnitude of the moment transcended time itself.

What is true is that the Union won the battle strategically, and this "win" enabled the president shortly after the battle to issue a preliminary Emancipation Proclamation freeing the slaves, and a formal proclamation January 1, 1863, changing the course of history.

Respectfully,

Patricia Polacco

Bibliography

Brands, H. W. *Lincoln's Genius*. Leesburg, Va.: Weider History Group, Inc., 2009.

Collins, Susan, and Jane Ammeson, in cooperation with the Marshall Historical Society. *Images of America: Marshall*. Charleston, S.C.: Arcadia Publishing, 2007.

Miller, William J., and Brian C. Pohanka. *An Illustrated History of the Civil War: Images of an American Tragedy*. Fairfax, Va.: Direct Holdings Americas Inc., 2000; New York: Barnes & Noble, 2006.

Pardoe, Debbie, and Susan Collins. *Postcard History Series: Marshall*. Charleston, S.C.: Arcadia Publishing, 2008.

Savas, Theodore P. *Brady's Civil War Journal: Photographing the War 1861–65*. New York: Colin Gower Enterprises Ltd., Skyhorse Publishing, 2008.

www.civilwar.org/battlefields/antietam.html
www.ohiohistorycentral.org

Patricia Lee Gauch, Editor

PUFFIN BOOKS
An imprint of Penguin Young Readers Group
Published by the Penguin Group
Penguin Group (USA) Inc.
375 Hudson Street
New York, New York 10014, U.S.A.

USA / Canada / UK / Ireland / Australia / New Zealand / India / South Africa / China
Penguin Books Ltd, Registered Offices: 80 Strand, London WC2R 0RL, England

For more information about the Penguin Group visit www.penguin.com

First published in the United States of America by G. P. Putnam's Sons, a division of Penguin Young Readers Group, 2011
Published by Puffin Books, an imprint of Penguin Young Readers Group, 2014

THE LIBRARY OF CONGRESS HAS CATALOGED THE G. P. PUTNAM'S SONS EDITION AS FOLLOWS:
Polacco, Patricia.
Just in time, Abraham Lincoln / Patricia Polacco.
p. cm.
Summary: When two brothers visit a museum in Harper's Ferry, West Virginia, with their grandmother, they find themselves in a very realistic Civil War setting where they see the Antietam battlefield and meet historical figures from the aftermath of that momentous battle. Includes author's note on the Battle of Antietam.
ISBN 978-0-399-25471-0 (hardcover)
1. Lincoln, Abraham, 1809–1865—Juvenile fiction. 2. Lincoln, Abraham, 1809–1865—Fiction. 3. Antietam, Battle of, Md., 1862—Juvenile fiction. 4. Antietam, Battle of, Md., 1862—Fiction. 5. Brothers—Fiction. 6. Maryland—History—Civil War, 1861–1865—Juvenile fiction. 7. Maryland—History—Civil War, 1861–1865—Fiction. 8. United States—History—Civil War, 1861–1865—Fiction.
I. Title
Includes bibliographical references.
PZ7.P75186 Jtw 2011
2010023200

Puffin Books ISBN 978-0-14-751062-4

Manufactured in China

1 3 5 7 9 10 8 6 4 2

The publisher does not have any control over and does not assume any responsibility for author or third-party websites or their content.